My Daddy Snores

To my husband, Steven, whose snoring inspired
My Daddy Snores and made me a "Musical Beds" expert!—N.H.R.

Affectionately for my Grandma Jessie.
She could really make the walls shake.—S.G.

ISBN-13: 978-0-545-02834-9
ISBN-10: 0-545-02834-5

16 15 14   11/0

Printed in the U.S.A.
This edition first printing, May 2007

My Daddy Snores

by Nancy H. Rothstein
Illustrated by Stephen Gilpin

Z Z Z Z Z Z

Scholastic Inc.
New York   Toronto   London   Auckland   Sydney
Mexico City   New Delhi   Hong Kong   Buenos Aires

On Monday, Daddy's snore boomed like a dinosaur's roar. The windows rattled. The walls trembled. So...

...Mommy played "Musical Beds."

She tried sleeping in my bed, but I hogged the blanket.
She tried sleeping in Natalie's crib, but it *broke!*

On Tuesday, Daddy's snore rum**bl**ed like an earthquake. It shook Mommy right out of bed! **So...**

But the faucet dripped water on her head...
all night long....

...Mommy slept in Hammy's cage.
But she was too squished. And it smelled **funny.**

On Thursday, Daddy's snore **buzzzzed** like a bumblebee. So...

...Mommy slept in the doghouse.

Aroooo!!

NO
SNORING
ZONE

But poor Rover didn't sleep a wink!
He howled instead...very **loudly!**

On Friday, Daddy's snore whistled like a teapot.
So this time...

...Mommy made Daddy sleep in Splishy's bowl.
But even Daddy's bubbles snored **loudly !**

It wasn't fair to Splishy at all.

On Saturday, Daddy's **snore** honked like a truck. Mommy had a great idea!

She made Daddy sleep in our tent.

But he **Woke UP** all the birds.

Then the birds **woke** *us* **up!**
It was not a great idea, after all.

On Sunday morning, Mommy looked like
a **zombie** having a bad hair day.
"No more **snoring!**" she yelled.

She took Daddy to the doctor. And the doctor helped to cure Daddy's **snoring.**

zzzz

On Sunday night,
Daddy didn't snore.
Our whole house was quiet.

Mommy slept. I slept.
Natalie slept.
Rover and Splishy
and Hammy slept.
Until...

...Daddy started talking in his sleep!

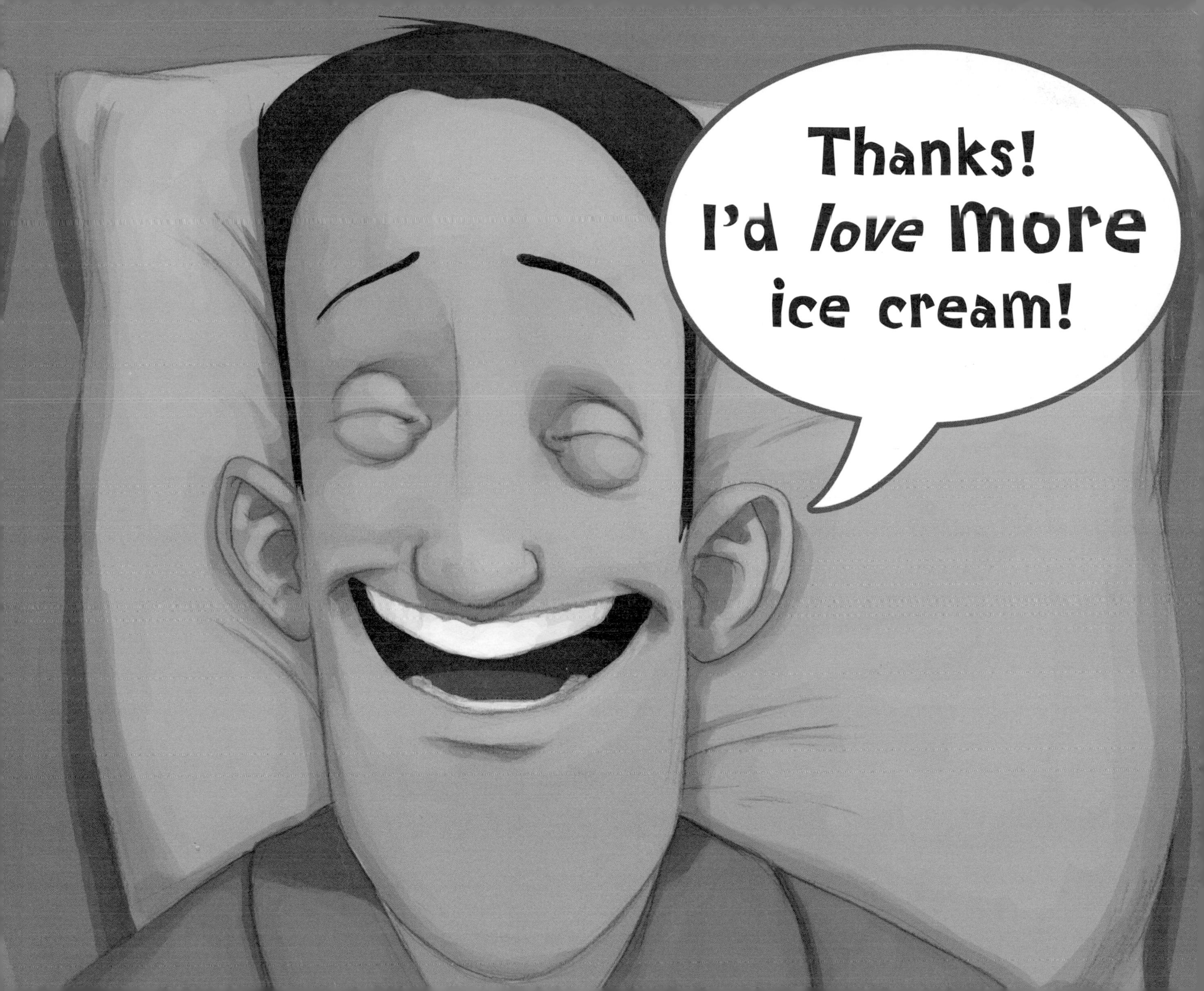
Thanks! I'd *love* more ice cream!

AFTERWORD Michael L. Gelb, D.D.S., M.S.

My Daddy Snores brings to light a problem that has an impact on tens of millions of households. When snoring is present, the whole family can be affected. Snoring can be a significant disturbance to sleep for both the person snoring, as well as those in ear's range of the noise.

Snorers should seek a medical professional for diagnosis as snoring may be indicative of serious health risks such as sleep apnea. Fortunately there are solutions and treatments for those who snore as prescribed by physicians, dentists, and sleep specialists. Based on a medical professional's diagnosis, treatments may range from weight loss, to positional sleeping, to oral appliances, to ENT surgery, and to a device called CPAP. Treatment for snoring continues to evolve.

While *My Daddy Snores* is playful and whimsical, identifying the underlying causes of snoring and obtaining a diagnosis are very important. The references listed at right provide information on snoring and related conditions so you can find out how to get help if snoring is a problem for you, your family, or your friends.

ORGANIZATIONS

American Academy of Sleep Medicine
One Westbrook Corporate Center, Suite 920
Westchester, IL 60154
(708) 492-0930
www.aasmnet.org
www.sleepeducation.com

American Academy of Dental Sleep Medicine
One Westbrook Corporate Center, Suite 920
Westchester, IL 60154
(708) 273-9366
www.dentalsleepmed.org

American Sleep Apnea Association
1424 K Street NW, Suite 302
Washington, DC 20005
(202) 293-3650
www.sleepapnea.org

National Sleep Foundation
1522 K Street NW, Suite 500
Washington, DC 20005
(202) 347-3471
www.sleepfoundation.org

BOOKS

Dement, William C., *The Promise of Sleep: A Pioneer in Sleep Medicine Explains the Vital Connection Between Health, Happiness, and a Good Night's Sleep.* New York: Delacorte Press, 1999.

Lavie, Peretz, *Restless Nights—Understanding Snoring and Sleep Apnea.* New Haven, CT: Yale University Press, 2003.

Johnson, T. Scott, *Sleep Apnea: The Phantom of the Night.* Onset, MA: New Technology Publishing, 2003.

Walsleben, Joyce, and Rita Baron-Faust, *A Woman's Guide to Sleep: Guaranteed Solutions for a Good Night's Rest.* New York: Three Rivers Press, 2001.

WEBSITES

www.mydaddysnores.com
www.quietsleep.com
www.sleepapneainfo.com
www.talkaboutsleep.com